THE ANIMALS
OF FARMER JONES

Illustrated by RUDOLF FREUND

A GOLDEN BOOK • NEW YORK

THE LITTLE GOLDEN BOOKS
ARE PREPARED UNDER THE SUPERVISION OF
MARY REED, Ph.D.
ASSISTANT PROFESSOR OF EDUCATION
TEACHERS COLLEGE, COLUMBIA UNIVERSITY

A COMMEMORATIVE FACSIMILE EDITION PUBLISHED ON THE OCCASION OF
THE 50TH ANNIVERSARY OF LITTLE GOLDEN BOOKS

It is supper time on the farm.
The animals are very hungry.
But where is Farmer Jones?

The horse stamps in his stall.
"Neighh, neighh," says the horse,
"I want my supper."
But where is Farmer Jones?

The cow jangles the bell round
her neck.
"Moo, moo," says the cow,
"I am very hungry."

And the calf kicks over the pail.
But where is Farmer Jones?

The sheep sniff in the corners
  of the barn.
"Ba-a-a, ba-a-a-a," say the sheep.
"We're waiting for supper."
But where is Farmer Jones?

"Cluck, cluck," say the hen and
the rooster. "Give us our supper."
"Yes, yes," say the little chicks
running after their mother.
"Our supper, our supper."
But where is Farmer Jones?

The turkey fluffs her feathers.
"Gobble, gobble," says the turkey.
"My food!   My food!"
But where is Farmer Jones?

The duck waddles out of the pond.
"Quack, quack," says the duck.
"Supper time, supper time."
But where is Farmer Jones?

The dog runs about barking.
"Wuff, wuff," says the dog.
"I want my meal."
But where is Farmer Jones?

The cat rubs against a chair
   in the kitchen.
"Me-o-w, me-o-w," says the cat.
"My dish is empty."
But where is Farmer Jones?

The pig sniffles and snuffles
in the trough.
"Oink, oink," says the pig.
"There's nothing to eat."

The baby pigs run round and round
in the pen.
"Oink, oink," say the baby pigs.
"Nothing to eat, nothing to eat."
But where is Farmer Jones?

WHERE IS FARMER JONES?

Farmer Jones is looking at his watch
  in the field.

"Six o'clock!" says Farmer Jones.

"It's supper time!"

Farmer Jones fills his wheelbarrow with supper for all the animals.   He takes

oats for the horse,
grain for the cows,
turnips for the sheep,
corn for the chickens,
wheat for the turkey,
barley for the duck,
bones for the dog,
milk for the cat,
mush for the pigs.

Farmer Jones gives oats to the horse.
"Nei-g-hh, nei-g-hh," says the horse.
"Thank you, Farmer Jones."

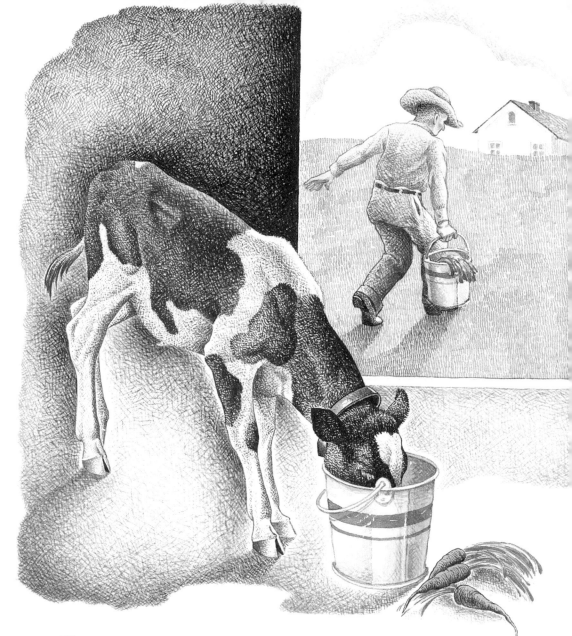

Farmer Jones gives grain to the cow.
"Moo, moo," says the cow.

"Thank you, Farmer Jones."

Farmer Jones gives turnips to the sheep.

"Ba-a-a, ba-a-a," say the sheep.

"Thank you, Farmer Jones."

Farmer Jones gives corn to the chickens.

"Cluck, cluck," say the chickens.

"Thank you, Farmer Jones."

Farmer Jones gives wheat to the turkey.
"Gobble, gobble," says the turkey.
"Thank you, Farmer Jones."

Farmer Jones gives barley to the duck.
"Quack, quack," says the duck.
"Thank you, Farmer Jones."

Farmer Jones gives bones to the dog.
"Wuff, wuff," says the dog.
"Thank you, Farmer Jones."

Farmer Jones gives milk to the cat.
"Me-e-o-w, me-e-o-w," says the cat.
"Thank you, Farmer Jones."

Farmer Jones gives mush to the pigs.
But the pigs don't say thank you.
The pigs don't say anything.
They are much too busy eating.

Good-by, Farmer Jones.